This picture dictionary is an interesting and enjoyable way of intro-ducing any young reader to words in everyday use – words that need to become part of the modern child's growing vocabulary.

The use of colorful, fun pictures accompanied by simply constructed sentences will delight any young reader and will, at the same time, help them to recognize, learn and remember a variety of different

A humorous and light-hearted approach has been used in both the illustrations and the text. We hope that this will capture children's interest and stimulate their desire to read and develop their skills in writing and spelling. This is a book to dip into again and again to really learn a lot about words, or simply have fun.

Copyright © 2010 Flowerpot Press.

a division of Kamalu LLC, Franklin, TN U.S.A. and Mitso Media, Inc., Oakville ON, Canada

American Edition Editor: Sean Kennelly

Printed in China.

THE FUN-TO-LEARN
PICTURE
DICTIONARY

▼

More than 1300 words explained
together with 850 color illustrations

A a

able
If you are able to do something – you can do it. I am able to read this dictionary, are you?

above
The sky is above the land. Above is opposite of below. The land is below the sky.

accident
An accident happens by chance and is always unexpected.

acrobats
Acrobats are very good at balancing tricks. You can see them performing on stage or in the circus.

across
When you walk across the road, you cross from one side to the other. Take care!

address
Your address is where you live. Write clearly when you address an envelope. This helps the postman deliver it to the correct address.

MISS JOLLYOEAN
21 THE AVENUE
POPULAR TOWN
MIOSHIRE MO62PQ

adult
An adult is a grown-up, not a child.

advertisement
An advertisement tells you about something for sale. 'Ads' are often seen on television, in newspapers and sometimes on the side of a bus.

airplane
A machine with wings that travels through the air, flown by a pilot. It is often called a 'plane'.

afraid
When you feel afraid, you are scared.

after
1. After can mean later on. Will you wash-up after you play?
2. It can also mean following behind. The fox ran after the goose.

again
To do something once more. Do your homework again!

against
1. He was standing against the fence. He was next to it.
2. It can mean opposed to. Tom is against washing!

age
How many years have you lived? This is your age.

agree
To think the same as other people. We all agree your hat is too big.

ahead
Ahead means in front of. Go ahead and I'll follow.

air
Air is all around. It is a mixture of gases we must breathe to live.

aircraft
The name for different kinds of machines that fly.

747-Jumbo

Concorde

Helicopter

Fighter

airport
The place where aircraft take off and land with cargo and passengers.

alarm
An alarm attracts attention. It is often a warning signal.

alike
Things that look or are the same.

all
All the mice are washing-up. That means every one of them.

allow
Allow is to let someone do something. Are you allowed to do that?

alone
No one is with me. I'm all alone.

alphabet
Here are the twenty-six of the alphabet.

ABCDEFGH
KLMNOPQR
TUVWXYZ

alive
Animals, plants and pec are all alive. They are living things.

also
Also means as well. I have a hamster. I also have a gold fish.

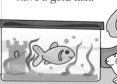

always
same at all times. The [su]n always rises in the morning.

ambulance
[Sic]k or injured people are [ru]shed to hospital in an ambulance.

an
[Yo]u use this tiny word [inste]ad of a, when the word [be]gins with a, e, i, o, or u.

[elep]hant

and
[An]d joins words together. [...]and John and Mary are pulling faces.

angry
[If] you are angry you feel [ver]y mad about something.

annoy
To make someone cross or tease them. John was beginning to annoy his dad.

another
Tell me another story means tell me one more.

answer
When we are asked a question, we must give an answer or reply.

any
Any can mean some, every or even one. It is often fixed in front of other words.

anyone
Is anyone there?

anything
Do you have anything to tell me?

anywhere
I can't find my glasses anywhere!

appetite
When you really want to eat and your dinner smells good, it gives you an appetite.

apron
An apron tied round you protects you from getting in a mess.

aquarium
A glass tank full of water for plants and fish.

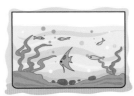

archer
Someone who shoots arrows from a bow. It is called archery.

area
The area is the size of a space or surface.

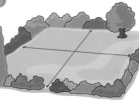

arithmetic
Using numbers to add, subtract, multiply and divide.

around
How would you like to fly around the world?

arrive
To reach a place is to arrive. The bus will arrive at ten o'clock.

artist
Famous artists make works of art when they draw and paint.

ask
Do you want to know something? Then just ask!

asleep
Grandpa is asleep in his chair. Soon he will be awake.

astronaut
An astronaut is a person who travels in space.

athlete
A person who trains hard to be good at sports and games.

atlas
A book full of maps.

attack
To attack is to begin to fight.

awake
I can't sleep, I am still wide awake!

away
The baby birds have flown away. They are no longer here.

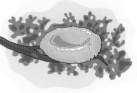

author
An author writes books, plays and stories.

autumn
The season after summer and before winter when crops are harvested.

B b

baby
A baby is a very young child.

back
1. Back means behind, opposite of front. Go to the back of the line!
2. I fell off the stool and hurt my back.

animal
Every living creature is an animal

Monkey

Snake

Rhino

Frog

Humans

Deer

Lion

B b

backwards
When you are on a swing, and you swing back, you are moving backwards.

bad
Bad means not good. Uncle is in a bad mood; he has a bad cold.

badge
Badges are worn by soldiers, scouts and members of clubs. Do you collect badges?

bag
Bags are containers for holding things and carrying them around.

bake
To cook food in a hot oven. The baker bakes bread and cakes.

balance
To hold something or yourself steady.

balloon
Balloons float when blown up, because they are filled with air.

bank
I. A mound of earth, a river-bank or sand-bank.

2. A building where your money is safely locked away.

barbecue
Cooking over a hot grill outdoors.

bare
If you are bare, you have nothing on. If the cupboard is bare, there is nothing in it.

bark
1. The noise made by a dog. Woof, woof!
2. The rough skin covering a tree.

barn
A farm building used for storage.

barrel
A large wooden tub to store food and drink.

base
The bottom of something. The part it stands on.

baseball
A favorite American team-game using a bat and ball

bath
You can put your whole self in the bath. Remember to wash behind your ears!

battery
A battery stores small amounts of electricity. All these things run on batteries.

beach
The beach is the strip of sand at the edge of the sea.

bead
A little ball with a hole pierced through. You thread beads on a string to make a necklace.

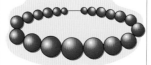

beak
A bird's bill or mouth. They all look very different.

beard
Hair that grows on a man's face and chin.

beat
1. Beat is to hit over and over again.
2. It can also mean to win. I can beat you at tennis!

2. It can mean in front Who is standing before drawbridge?

begin
To begin with is anoth way of saying to start v Begin the book at the beginning!

believe
Do you believe in stor about fairies? Do you th they are true?

bell
There are many differe kinds of bells. They ma ringing noise.

below
Below means undernea A mole digs tunnels be the ground.

belt
A thin strip of leathe or plastic fastened rou your waist.

bend
1. A curve in the road called a bend.
2. A strong man can be an iron bar.

beneath
Another word for low than. The earth is bene the sky.

berry
Small juicy fruits with seeds. Some are good to some are poisonous.

Strawberry   *Blackbe*

Gooseberry

Blackcurrants

best
Susan's cake is best. It better than all the res

between
The middle of two things.

beyond
The rainbow is beyond the hills. It is far away, out of reach.

bicycle
A bike has two wheels and is pedalled along by the rider.

big
An elephant is big, but a whale is bigger. It is the biggest mammal in the world.

A blue whale can 10 times heavier than an elephant . . .

and up to 100 feet long

billiards (pool)
A game played on a special table with balls and cues.

binoculars
A telescope made with two eyes. Binoculars make things seem nearer.

bird
All birds have wings and feathers and most of them can fly.

Goose

Owl

Robin

Penguin

Duck

Cuckoo

Swallow

Ostrich

Heron

birthday
Your birthday is the day you were born.

biscuit
A crunchy flat kind of cookie. Yum! Yum!

bit
A little piece or fragment of a bigger thing.

---

bite
To bite is to cut into something with your teeth.

bitter
Bitter tastes sharp. A lemon is bitter.

blackboard
Every school has a blackboard. You write on it with chalk.

blanket
A soft warm cover. In winter you snuggle under the blankets.

blizzard
A blinding storm with wind and driving snow.

blood
Red liquid in your veins. Cut a finger and it bleeds.

blossom
A flower is a blossom. Some blossom comes before fruit; apple, pear and cherry blossom.

blow
1. Blow is to make the air move. The wind blows.
2. It can mean a smack or a hard knock.

blush
When you blush your face turns pink.

---

boat
A boat floats on water. Some have sails and oars, others have engines.

Rowing boat

Sailing boat

Speedboat

body
The whole of you is your body.

boil
When water is heated it bubbles up and boils. The kettle's boiling!

Water boils at 220°F

bone
Your skeleton is made up of all the bones inside your body.

bonfire
You light a bonfire outside in the garden.

---

book
A book is a collection of sheets of paper bound together. Usually a book contains words and pictures.

boomerang
An Australian weapon like a curved stick. When you throw it, it comes back.

borrow
To ask someone for something for a little while. Can I borrow your tie?

bottle
A container for holding liquids. You can pour easily from a bottle.

bottom
The lowest part of something. The treasure is at the bottom of the sea.

bounce
When you bounce you spring up and down again and again.

bouquet
A bunch of flowers nicely wrapped.

bow
1. There's a bow of ribbon round the box.

2. When you bend over from the waist you bow.

3. Robin Hood shot arrows from a bow.

bowl
A hollow, deep dish.

boy
A boy is a young, male child who will grow up to be a man.

bracelet
A piece of jewellery worn round your wrist.

branch

The branches are the arms of a tree; they spread out from the trunk.

bread
Bread is made of flour, water and yeast, left to rise, then baked in the oven.

1. Break is to smash to pieces.
2. It can also mean a pause. Take a break!

breath
Breath is the air you draw in and blow out of your lungs.

brick
A block of clay that has been baked, then used to build walls.

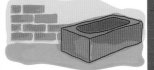

bridge
A bridge is a road built over a gap so people can cross.

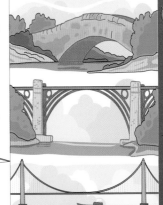

bright
Ben is sitting in the bright sun in his bright yellow shorts. The opposite of dark.

bring
Bring is to fetch or carry back. The opposite of take. Bring me my supper!

broken
My leg is broken. I must be careful not to break the other one.

broom
A long-handled sweeping brush.

brought
When the giant shouted for his supper, his wife brought it at once.

brush
A handle with hairs or bristles. What a lot of brushes we all use!

bubble
A transparent ball of liquid, filled with gas and air, that floats.

bucket
You can fill a bucket with water and carry it.

bud
A flower or leaf before it opens.

build
To build is to make something by putting several things together.

bulb
1. An electric light bulb lights up when it is switched on.
2. A flower bulb grows below the soil and flowers in spring.

bulldozer
A big earthmoving tractor with a blade at the front.

bump
When you knock or jolt something you bump it.

bungalow
A house with all the rooms on one floor.

bunk
A bunk is a bed in a ship's cabin. Have you ever slept in bunk beds?

burglar
Someone who breaks into your house to steal things.

burn
If you set fire to paper it will burn. Be careful not to burn your fingers.

burst
Prick a balloon with a pin and it will burst.

bus
A bus carries lots of passengers around. Some buses are double-deckers. You go upstairs to the top deck.

bush
A small tree or shrub, like a rose bush.

butcher
A man who cuts meat into pieces to sell for cooking.

butter
Cream that is churned or whipped until it thickens into butter.

buy
To buy is to pay money for something. Once you have bought it, it is yours.

C

cab
A taxi or car where you pay the driver for a ride.

cactus
A prickly desert plant.

cage
Animals and birds are often kept in a cage. Bars on the sides keep them in.

cake
Make a cake, then bake a cake. This is a birthday cake.

calculator
A machine that can add, subtract, divide and multiply.

calendar
A calendar shows you the days and dates in each month of the year.

call
This word can mean lots of things.
"I am going to call my baby Sophie."
"I must make a phone call."
"Call out if you need me."

camera
A machine for taking photographs.

Video camera

camp
You camp outdoors in a tent at a campsite.

candle
A stick of wax with a wick down the middle. It burns when you light it.

cannon
A very big gun.

Some cannons are mounted on wheels.

canoe
A light, narrow boat you in and paddle.

capital
1. A large letter of the alphabet.
2. A capital city is the ma city of a country.

captain
1. The captain is in char of a ship.
2. The team captain is t leader of the team.

car
A motor vehicle with a engine and four wheels used to carry people.

card
A stiff piece of paper wit art like a birthday card.

carpet
A deep, soft material covering the floor.

carry
The waiter carried the tra He took it from one place another.

cartoon
A funny drawing or a sho film made with comic characters.

BIRTHDAY CHARLIE

cassette
A small flat box that contains the tape for a video or tape recorder.

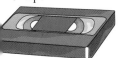

castle
A home for kings and noblemen, with thick, stone towers to keep their enemies out.

centimeter
One hundred centimeters equal one meter.

center
The middle of something.

century
A century is one hundred years.

cereal
Corn, barley, rice, wheat and oats are all cereals.

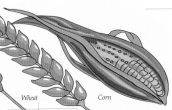

Oats *Barley* *Wheat* *Corn*

cheap
Cheap things cost less money.

cheer
To shout and make a noise when your team is winning.

choose
Choose is to pick. Can you choose the biggest ice cream?

chop
Chop means to cut into pieces or to cut down.

city
A very large town is called a city.

clap
To strike your hands together. When an audience claps it is called applause.

class
A group of people learning things together.

classroom
A room where the class meets for lessons.

clay
Wet, soft, sticky earth that is made into pots or bricks and baked hard.

caterpillar
A grub which becomes a pupa, then turns into a butterfly or moth.

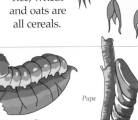

Pupa

certain
To be certain is to be sure. I am certain four comes before five!

chain
Rings linked together in a row.

chair
A seat for one person. Baby Bear had a tiny chair.

champion
Champion is another word for winner.

chance
1. It happened by chance means just by luck.
2. Give me a chance to win!

change
To make something different. He changed his hairstyle.

chase
To run after

cheese
A food made from milk. It has a savory taste and is good for you.

chemist
Someone who makes things with chemicals.

chest
1. A strong box.
2. You puff out your chest when you take a deep breath.

chief
Chief means leader. It can also mean the most important.

child
A child is a young boy or girl. Fred and Freda are children.

chimney
A chimney takes the smoke away from the fire.

chocolate
A hot drink or a variety of delicious candies.

choir
A group of singers, often singing hymns in church.

Christmas
This is the time that people celebrate the birth of Jesus.

church
People pray and worship in a building called a church.

circle
A perfectly round figure like a ring.

circumference
The distance round a circle.

circus
A travelling show with clowns, animals and acrobats.

clean
Clean is well washed and not dirty at all.

cliff
A cliff is a steep rockface. Do not go near the edge!

climate
The different kinds of weather in all sorts of places.

clock
An instrument that measures and tells us the time.

cattle
Some cattle are wild like buffalo. Others are domesticated like our cows.

ceiling
This is the top of a room, the floor is the bottom.

cellar
A room under the house.

close
1. Close means to shut. Close that window, It's cold!

2. It can also mean near. Sit close by me, I feel lonely!

clothes
All sorts of different things to wear made of cloth.

cloud
A cloud is made up of tiny drops of water floating together in the sky.

clumsy
A clumsy person is awkward, and bumps into things.

coach
A coach is a teacher or trainer.

coal
A hard, black rock dug out of the ground that burns.

coast
Where the land meets the sea.

cobweb
A spider spins a silken cobweb to trap insects.

coconut
A huge, hairy nut that grows high up in a palm tree.

coffee
Coffee beans are roasted and ground up. Add boiling water and you have a lovely cup of coffee.

coin
A piece of money made of metal.

cold
It is always cold in winter. Now is the time you catch a cold.

collar
A shirt collar fits around your neck. The dog has a collar round his neck too.

collect
Collect means to gather together.

color
There are many colors, here are just a few.

come
To come means to move near and not go away.

comma
A comma is a punctuation mark. It divides two parts of a sentence.

compare
You notice if things are alike or different, you compare them.

compass
You can find your way if you have a compass. The needle always points north.

complete
Complete has nothing missing. This puzzle is complete.

computer
A machine that can store, process and give out large amounts

of information at great speed.

concert
A musical performance given by an orchestra, band and sometimes a choir.

cone
A cone is round and flat at the bottom and goes to a point at the top.

connect
Connect means to join together.

construct
Construct is to make or build. Boys love construction toys.

continent
A large mass of land. The Earth is made up of seas and continents.

cook
A person that makes a meal to eat. I cooked the breakfast this morning!

cool
Cool feels a little bit warmer than cold. On a hot day the water feels cool.

copy
To make something that is exactly like another.

corner
A street corner is where two streets meet. Two straight lines meeting make a corner.

correct
Right, with no mistakes at all.

cosmonaut
A Russian spaceman.

costume
Putting on a costume means dressing up. In some countries a national costume is worn.

Mexico

Japan

Lapland

cottage
A little house in the cou... Here is a thatched cottage.

count
To count is to add up h... many there are.

country
1. When you leave tov... and begin to see field... you are in the countr...
2. A country is a land a... all its people, America... Spain; China.

cover
"Cover me up in b... With my pretty, blu... blanket."

cowboy
A man in charge of herd... cattle on a ranch.

crab
A crab is a sea creature w... a hard shell and two clav... like pincers.

crack
1. A sharp noise like the... crack of thunder.
2. A very fine break. This cup is cracked!

cradle
A bed for a baby.

crash
1. A sudden fall which... makes a loud noise.
2. An accident when peop... or things are smashed.

crawl
To move around on you... hands and knees.

crayon
colored, wax stick for drawing pictures.

creature
ll living things except plants.

crime
rong deed. This burglar as committed a crime.

cross
These lines n the shape f a cross.
2. When we are cross we feel angry.
Cross the road with care.

crowd
ny people all together in one place.

crown
The hats of kings d queens, made of gold and jewels.

cry
When you cry, tears fall from your eyes.
When you cry for help, you shout loudly.

cube
olid shape with six equal square sides.

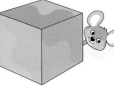

curtain
oths that cover windows or the front of a stage.

curve
A bent line that has no straight part.

cushion
soft, fat pillow usually on a chair.

---

customer
A person who goes into a shop to buy something.

cut
To divide into pieces with scissors, a knife or a saw.

cycle
Another word for bicycle. I cycled down the street.

cylinder
A shape like a tube. It can be solid or hollow.

daily
Daily is every day. The newspaper is delivered daily.

dairy
Milk is kept at the dairy. Often cheese, butter and yogurt are made there.

damage
The storm caused a lot of damage, it did a lot of harm.

damp
Damp means slightly wet. Babies are sometimes damp!

dance
Dance is to move around to music. The waltz is a dance.

---

danger
Danger is something harmful. How very dangerous!

dark
Dark means no light. Witches go out on dark nights, dressed in dark clothes.

date
The date tells you the day, the month and the year.

daughter
The female child with parents.

day
A day lasts twenty four hours. There are seven days in a week.

decide
If you make up your mind, you decide.

deck
The deck is the floor of a ship.

decorate
When you decorate a room for a party, you make it look pretty.

deep
Deep goes a long way down. In Switzerland the snow can be very deep.

---

deli
A shop selling cooked meats and cheeses from different countries.

delicious
Something good to eat tastes delicious.

deliver
When the postman delivers the letters, he hands them over to you.

dentist
The dentist takes care of your teeth.

describe
To write or tell someone about something.

desert
A land where there is very little water and nothing can grow.

desk
A little table which sometimes has a sloping top. You sit at a desk to write and read at school.

detective
A person who tries to solve a crime.

---

detergent
We use all kinds of detergents when we are spring cleaning. They help clean the dirt.

diagram
A drawing or plan that helps explain things.

Kitchen 7'6"x7'4"   Storage 5'2"x4'4"   Bath 4'5"x7'10"
Living room 12'6"x12'   Bedroom 9'x11'

diamond
A very hard precious stone. It has to be cut and polished before it is made into jewellery.

diary
A daily record of events.

You make notes in your diary as a reminder.

dictionary
A book that tells you the meaning of words.

different
Different means not the same. Can you spot the difference?

difficult
A difficult thing is hard to do, not easy.

dig
You dig the earth with a shovel. A machine called a digger can dig deeper and faster.

dinosaur
These great reptiles lived on Earth millions of years ago. Now they are all gone.

draw
You use a pencil, a crayon or chalks to draw. Who drew that?

drawer
An open box that slides in and out of furniture.

dry
Dry has no wet at all. Rub the baby dry, then hang the towel out to dry!

during
During the storm I hid under the bed. During means while it lasted.

earth
1. We live on a planet called Earth.

2. Another name for so

earthquake
When the ground shak and cracks open.

direction
The way in which you go. You're going in the wrong direction!

doctor
A doctor looks after people who are ill.

dirty
If you need a bath, you are dirty.

dolphin
Dolphins are intelligent and playful creatures. They swim very fast in groups, then suddenly leap out of the water high into the air.

dye
If you dye a garment or your hair, you change the colour by using different dyes that stain.

disappear
If something has disappeared, it has vanished and can't be found.

discover
This means to find something. Christopher Columbus discovered America.

dome
A dome has a shape like half an orange. A dome is usually placed on top of a building.

dream
The thoughts that come into your head when you are asleep.

drink
To drink is to swallow a liquid. What would you like to drink?

E e

Happy Easter

disguise
A disguise changes the look of something or somebody!

door
To enter a room or building you have to go in through the door.

drive
1. To drive is to make any vehicle travel along.
2. When the farmer drives his geese into the pens, he makes them go inside.

each
Each means every one. Each dog has a spot!

easel
A stand for a painting or a blackboard.

east
The sun rises in the east China and Japan are to t east of the map.

dish
A dish is a shallow bowl or plate like a pie dish.

double
1. Double is twice as much.
2. Do you have a double? – someone who looks just like you.

distance
Distance is the space between two things or places.

down
Down means to go lower. Get down from that ladder!

3. The drive is the road leading up to a house.

eager
If you are eager, you really want to do something.

easy
Easy things are simple understand or do. Nev hard or difficult.

dive
To jump or fall head first into something. You dive into the water and you make a dive for the ball.

dragon
Dragons can be found in fairy tales and legends.

drop
1. To drop is to let something fall.
2. It also means a little blob of liquid.

ear
People and animals hear with their ears.

eat
When you eat you put fo into your mouth, chew then swallow.

do
Do is to carry out a thing. Busy people are doing things all day long!

drown
If you sink below the waves and breathe in water instead of air, you drown.

early
Get there before it starts, be early!

echo
A sound which bounce back again and again fro the walls of mountains or caves.

edge
The end or side of something. Don't fall off the edge!

egg
Birds and a few animals have inside eggs before they hatch.

either
Either means one or the other of two things. You can have either a cake or a carrot.

electricity
Electricity is power that reaches us along wires. Many machines run on electric power.

emergency
When something very unexpected happens and you need help.

empty
Empty has nothing in it. My bag was full but now it's empty!

encyclopedia
A book or several books that contain information on most subjects.

end
The last part or finish of something. This is the end!

THE END

engine
The engine makes the power that drives the machine.

enormous
Enormous is very, very big. Do giants have enormous feet?

enough
As much as you need and no more. Have you had enough?

enter
When you enter, you go in. You can enter a room. You can also enter a competition.

envelope
A folded paper cover usually for a letter.

equal
Things that are equal are the same in size and value.

equator
The imaginary line round the center of the Earth.

escalator
A moving staircase often in a store or hotel.

escape
To get away, be free. My beetles have escaped!

even
1. An even number can be divided by two.
2. An even surface is flat and smooth.

evening
The end of the day when the sun sets, before night.

ever
Ever means always. I will love you for ever!

every
Every means each one. We get older every minute.

everybody
Everybody means all people. Everybody is born!

everything
Everything means all things. Everything in the room was yellow.

everywhere
Here, there, everywhere; dust gets in all places.

exactly
This piece fits exactly. It is just right.

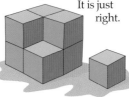

excellent
Excellent means very, very good. Your exam results are excellent!

excited
To be thrilled with pleasure about something. I am very excited about this trip!

exercise
1. Exercising your body keeps you fit.

2. Doing exercises on the flute helps you to play better.

exit
The way out.

EXIT

explain
"Can you tell me why you made such a mess?" Then you have to explain.

explode
When something bursts or blows up it explodes with a loud bang.

explore
You can explore a country by going through it and finding new places and things.

extinct
Something that has died out is extinct. The dodo is extinct.

DODO

extra
Extra means more than you have. I would like extra gravy on my meat!

extraordinary
Something that is very unusual.

eye
You have two eyes. They are used for seeing. If you have good eyesight, you are able to see well. If you lose your sight and cannot see, you are blind.

F f

FREE FLIGHTS ON FRIDAY

fable
A fable is a short story with a moral. Aesop wrote many famous fables.

face
At the front of your head under your hair is your face.

fact
A fact is something that can be proved to be true.

fail
To fail is to try but not manage to do something.

fairy
A tiny creature that is believed to be magic. Do you believe in fairies?

fall
Fall means to drop down. An apple has fallen on my head!

false
False means untrue or not real. Is he wearing a false nose?

family
Your family are people related to you.

far
Far is a long way off. The ship sailed far away.

farm
A farm is the land and buildings where crops are grown and animals kept.

farmer
The person who lives and works on the farm.

fast
Fast is very quick. A speedboat is faster than a rowing boat.

fasten
You must fasten your safety belt. If it is buckled you will be safe.

father
A father is the male parent of his children.

favorite
Favorite things are the things you like best.

fear
To fear is to feel you are in danger. Are you afraid of the dark?

feather
Feathers cover a bird's body. The large feathers help it to fly and the down helps the bird to keep warm.

feed
To feed is to give someone food. This robin is feeding her young.

feel
To feel something is to handle it and touch it.

fence
If you enclose your garden, you put up a fence as a barrier.

fern
A plant with feathery leaves. Ferns love cool shady places.

few
If you have a few sweets, there are not very many.

field
A piece of land for growing crops or grazing animals.

fierce
Some wild animals are savage and frightening. They are very fierce.

fight
When you fight you argue with someone and sometimes hit them.

figure
A figure is the shape of a number or a person.

fill
To leave no space for any more.

fine
1. A fine day is alway[s] warm and sunny.
2. A hair is fine. It is thin[like] a thread.

finger
Fingers are at the end[s] of your hands. You ha[ve] eight fingers and tw[o] thumbs.

fire
If something is on fire i[t is] burning. Send for the [fire] department! A fire eng[ine] will come as soon as possible. When the bla[ze is] put out the firefighters [will] return to the fire static[n.]

firework
You must treat firewor[ks] with care because the[y] explode. We all love fireworks on the 4th of J[uly.]

fish
A fish is a swimming an[imal] which lives in the wat[er.] They breathe underwa[ter] through their gills.

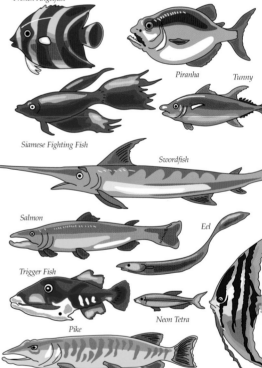

Shubunkin

French Angelfish

Piranha   *Tunny*

Siamese Fighting Fish

Swordfish

Salmon

Eel

Trigger Fish

Neon Tetra

Pike

film
1. A film is a moving picture at the movie theater or on television.
2. You take photographs on a film inside a camera.

find
To discover something that was lost, or that you didn't know was there.

fit
1. Keep fit, stay health[y.]
2. If your shoes do not [fit] they are either too big [or] too small.

fix
1. To mend or repair.
2. To influence somethi[ng] unfairly. That football ga[me] was fixed!

flag

piece of cloth with an [em]lem on it. Each country [h]as a flag of its own.

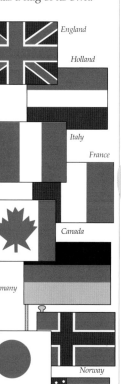

England

Holland

Italy

France

Canada

[Ger]many

Norway

[Jap]an

U.S.A.

floor

[We] walk on the floor. It is [the l]owest part of the room.

flour

[Fl]our is the soft, white [pow]der made from crushed grains of wheat.

flower

[Fl]owers are made up of [br]ightly colored petals, [insi]de which are the seeds.

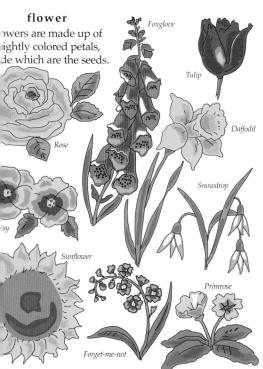

Foxglove

Tulip

Daffodil

Rose

Snowdrop

[Pan]sy

Sunflower

Primrose

Forget-me-not

fly

1. If you move through the air you fly. Many things fly all by themselves.
2. There is a tiny insect called a fly.

follow

"Follow me," said the fox, "I will lead and you can walk behind."

food

To stay alive we must eat food.

foot

The lowest part of your leg from your ankle to your toe is your foot.

forest

Lots of trees growing together in one big area.

forget

If you don't remember things, you forget them. Have you forgotten the time?

free

1. If a thing is free it costs nothing at all.

2. Prisoners are not free, they cannot come and go as they please.

freeze

When water freezes it gets very cold then turns to ice.

fresh

Fresh means new and clean. Food that is fresh has just been made or picked.

friend

A friend is someone you know very well and like a lot.

fright

What gives you a fright or scares you?

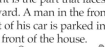

front

Front is the part that faces forward. A man in the front seat of his car is parked in front of the house.

fruit

The seeds of a plant grow inside the fruit.

Apple

Pear

Banana

Strawberry

Melon

Lemon

Peach

Cherries

Brazil nut

Gooseberry

Hazelnut

Blackberry

Orange

fry

When you fry food you cook it in hot fat or oil.

fun

You laugh when you are having fun.

fur

The hair that covers an animal's body is called fur.

furniture

Houses are full of furniture. We use it every day.

G g

gain

To gain is to increase. It is the opposite of lose.

gale

When there is a gale blowing, the wind is very strong.

gallery

You go to a gallery to see works of art.

game

In any game you play, you must keep to the rules.

garage

A place where cars are kept or repaired.

garden

A garden is a space, usually round a house, for growing flowers and vegetables. You can relax and play in your garden.

gate

A gate is an outside door in a wall, hedge or fence.

geese

A flock of geese is a lot of geese together. One bird on its own is a goose.

G g

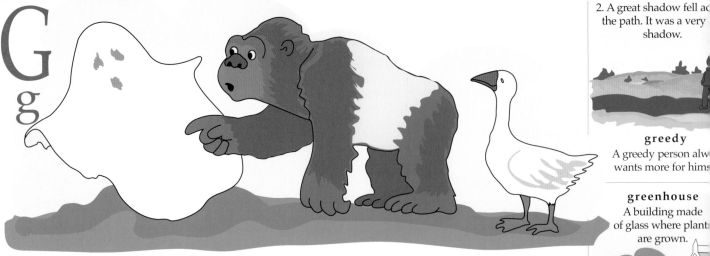

2. A great shadow fell ac
the path. It was a very
shadow.

greedy
A greedy person alw
wants more for hims

greenhouse
A building made
of glass where plant
are grown.

gentle
A gentle person is loving
and careful, not rough in
any way.

geography
In geography we learn all
about the Earth, the
animals, the people and the
way they all live.

germ
Germs are so tiny you can
only see them under a
microscope. They can
cause disease.

giant
A thing or person that is
huge. There are lots of
giants in fairy tales.

gift
A gift is a present,
something that is given.

girl
When your mother was
young she was a girl. A girl
grows up to be a woman.

give
If you give a thing away
you do not ask for it back.

glad
I am glad you came, means
I am very happy that you
came.

glass
You can see right through
glass. Although it is very
hard, it breaks easily.

globe
The globe is shaped like a
ball and has a map of the
world on its surface.

glove
Gloves cover your hands
and keep them warm.
They have a separate little
cover for each finger.

glue
You can stick things
together with glue.
It is often very sticky.

go
Go means to leave one place
for another. You go your
way, I'll go mine.

goal
To score a goal is the
purpose of some games.

gold
Gold is a very precious
yellow metal.

goggles
They fit tightly to your face and
protect your
eyes, so you
can still see
properly.

good
1. He is a good boy, he is
well behaved, not naughty.
2. Her work is very good.
It is first class!

goodbye
You say goodbye when you
are parting from someone.

govern
To govern is to rule
and guide people.
A government is a group
of people who promise
to do this.

grab
When you grab something
you catch hold of it
suddenly. I grabbed a bun
before mother grabbed me!

grandfather
My father's father and my
mother's father are my
grandfathers.

grandmother
My father's mother and my
mother's mother are my
grandmothers.

grass
Grass is green with thin
sword-shaped leaves.

great
1. Abraham Lincoln was a
great man. He was an
important man. He became
President of the United
States of America.

grin
A great big smile!

ground
Everyone walks on
the ground. It is the
Earth's surface.

grow
To grow is to get bigg
My how you've grow

guard
The soldiers are on gu
looking after the Queen
keeping her safe.

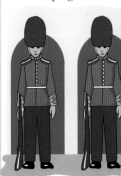

guardian
Someone who looks a
defends, or is responsi
for someone or someth

guess
[s]ay or think something [y]ou don't really know.

guide
[G]uide is to show the way. [G]uide-dogs lead blind people.

gun
[D]angerous weapon that fires bullets. [C]owboys carry guns.

gym
[L]arge room where people keep fit on special equipment.

H h

hair
Hair grows on the bodies of animals and humans. Some people are more hairy than others.

half
If you cut something in half you get two pieces of equal size. Each one is called a half.

Halloween
The thirty-first of October is Halloween, the night that witches fly about!

halt
When you are told to halt, you must stop moving at once!

hamburger
A round, flat patty of minced beef, often served in a bread bun.

handle
A hammer has a handle. Be careful how you handle it!

handwriting
The way you write with a pen or pencil.

Dear Jane,
Thank you for your letter. I was very happy to hear about your holiday.

happen
When something happens, it takes place. What happened to you?

happy
Full of joy and very pleased about things.

hard
1. Hard is difficult, not easy to do.
2. Hard also means solid and firm. Hard as iron!

harm
To do harm is to hurt or damage a person or thing.

harvest
To gather in all the crops when they are ready.

hat
You wear a hat to cover and protect your head.

hate
To hate is to really dislike a thing. I hate washing dishes!

have
If you have a thing, you own it. I have long hair now, when I was a baby I had none at all.

head
1. The top part of a person's or animal's body.
2. It can also mean the boss or most important thing or person.

health
Your health is how your body feels. Healthy is well, unhealthy is ill.

hear
You hear sounds through your ears when you listen.

heart
Your heart is like a pump that sends the blood round your body.

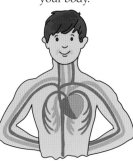

heat
Hot things give off heat.

heavy
Something heavy weighs a lot.

help
To help is to make things easier for another person. I will help you paint the fence!

hesitate
To be reluctant to do something or to hold back. She hesitated before climbing up the ladder.

hire
To employ someone to do some work.

hollow
A hollow has nothing empty space inside The magician showed us a hollow tube.

herbs
Each herb has a different smell and flavor. These plants are used for medicine and food.

Thyme

Mint

Parsley

Bay leaves

Basil   *Rosemary*

home
Home is where you live.

homework
Work brought from school to be done at home.

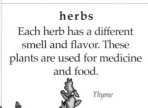

heel
The back of your foot or the back of your shoe is a heel.

height
Measure your height from the ground to the top of your head.

here
Here is the place you are at this moment. I live here!

hexagon
A six-sided shape.

hibernate
When the weather turns cold some animals hibernate and go to sleep for the winter.

his
His means belonging to a man. Is that jacket really his?

history
History is the story of the past. Learning history is often hard!

honest
To be honest is to be truthful.

hook
A bent piece of metal catching hold of thing

hop
To bob up and down on foot. Who is this hopp along?

helicopter
A helicopter is lifted up into the air and flies by its whirling blades.

hide
Will you hide him and keep him out of sight? See that he is well hidden!

high
Mountains are very high. They are a long way from the ground.

hit
Hit is to strike out or knock something or someone.

hope
I hope my wish wil come true! You really v your wish to happen

hello
Hello is a greeting. When you answer the telephone you say hello!

hero
A hero is a very brave man or boy.

hold
This box holds candy. Hold out your hand and you can have one!

horizon
The horizon is the pla where the ground and sky seem to meet.

helmet
A helmet is a hard hat which protects the head.

heroine
A heroine is a very brave woman or girl.

hill
A hill is a small mountain with gently sloping sides.

hint
To suggest, without saying something clearly. Joe's friend hinted that he would like to stay for dinner.

hole
A hole is an opening. It can go right through a thing, or it can form a hollow.

horn
The hard part that sticks out of an animal's head.

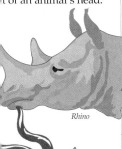
Rhino

Antelope

Deer

Have you a horn on your bicycle?

hospital
You have had an accident or you are ill you go to hospital to be taken care of.

hot
Do not touch hot things. They give off heat and could burn you.

hotel
When you are away from home, you can pay for a room and a meal in a hotel.

hour
Sixty minutes in one hour, twenty-four hours in a day.

hovercraft
A hovercraft carries passengers just above the sea or land on a cushion of air.

how
This is an asking word; how was that done?

human
People, because they think and speak, are human. Animals are not.

hungry
I am hungry. I need some food because I lost my lunch!

hurricane
A violent storm with strong winds that can cause a lot of damage.

hurry
To be quick or rush. Hurry up, or we will miss the bus!

hurt
Someone who is hurt is in pain. I bet that hurts!

hutch
A home for a pet rabbit.

hydrogen
A colorless gas, which combines with oxygen to make water.

hymn
A song of praise to God.

hypnosis
A trance-like state in which the person is open to suggestion.

I i

ice
Ice is frozen water. It is solid, cold and hard.

iceberg
An iceberg is a mountain of ice floating in the sea.

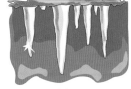

ice cream
Ice cream is cream and sugar frozen. If you lick it, it melts in your mouth.

icicle
A spike of ice hanging down where water has dripped and frozen into a point.

idea
When Sally has a clever idea, she has a clever thought in her mind.

ill
My brother feels unwell today. I'm sure he is ill.

immediately
"Take that make-up off immediately!" She means right now.

impossible
It is impossible to count all the grains of sand. It can't be done.

indoors
Table tennis is an indoor game, it is played inside.

infant
A very young child is an infant. It can be a boy or a girl.

injure
The skier hit a pine tree and was injured. He was hurt badly.

ink
Your pen is full of a colored liquid called ink.

insect
There are many different kinds of insects, all have six legs.

Butterfly

Moth

Ladybug

Stag beetle

Fly

Bumble-bee

Ant

Earwig

inside
You can be inside a room and inside the cupboard. You are not outside, you are within.

instant
Quick as a flash! In an instant, the wizard turned the frog into a prince.

instrument
Music is played on an instrument. Here are some of them.

Keyboard

Drum

Guitar

Trumpet

Violin

Triangle

Recorder

Tambourine

introduce
Baby Bear introduced the little girl to his Mommy and Daddy. "This is Goldilocks!" he said.

inventor
An inventor thinks of something useful that no one has ever thought of before.

invisible
Something invisible cannot be seen.

invite
To invite is to ask someone to do something. Here is an invitation to my party.

iron
1. A hard metal that is used to make steel.
2. I will iron your jeans with my new iron!

island
An island is land surrounded by water. Fiji is a small island, Australia is a huge one.

Australia

Fiji

2.
When things are squeezed tightly together they are jammed. These cars are in a traffic jam.

3.
A very fast airplan driven by a jet engine, propellers. The engin makes hot gases whi escape backwards ar thrust the plane forwa

jar
A jar is a container with a wide opening at the top. Jars often hold food.

jaw
The base of your mouth to which your teeth are fixed.

jealous
I am jealous because she won the cup. I want it, although it belongs to her!

jewel
A jewel is a precious st

J j

jacket
A jacket is a short coat. It can also mean a cover or an outer casing.

jail
When you are sent to prison you are put in jail.

jam
1. Jam is made by boiling sugar and fruit together.

jeans
Pants made from a thick, cotton cloth called denim.

jelly
Jelly is made from fruit juice and gelatin. When set, it is clear and wobbly.

jellyfish
A jellyfish drifts in the sea. Its body is like a jelly and it can sting you!

jet
1. A fast stream of liquid or gas.
2. A hard black stone.

jewelry
An ornament made of g and silver and jewels

jigsaw
A picture cut up into pie for you to fit together ag

job
This man is a milkma It is his jo delive m

jog

hen horses jog they trot
wly. People jog to keep
fit.

join

1. When you join two
hings, you fasten them
together.

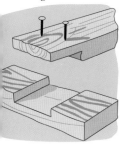

When you join a club you
become a member.
Join the Scouts!

joke

joke is a short story that
kes you laugh. Have you
heard this joke?

jolly

hen we hear lots of jokes
we feel jolly.

journey

hen you go on a journey
u travel to a place. It can
be a short or long trip.

joy

en you jump for joy, you
are delighted.

judge

person who decides what
right and what is wrong
in a dispute.

jug

A jug
holds
liquids and
is very easy
to pour

juggler

Jugglers entertain you by
balancing objects and
keeping them in the air at
the same time.

juice

The liquid squeezed from
fruit and vegetables.

jumbo

Anything very large,
often used to refer to
an elephant.

jump

Spring into the air with both
feet off the ground.

junction

The place where two or
more roads meet.

jungle

A jungle is a tropical forest,
it is dense and overgrown.

jury

The group of people who
decide whether or not
someone is guilty at a trial.
A jury can also be the
judges of a competition.

K k

keen

If you are keen, you are
very willing to do things.

keep

To keep is to hold onto
something. A miser keeps
all his money to himself.

ketchup

A thick, tasty sauce for food.

kettle

You boil water in a kettle.
It has a spout for pouring
out the water.

key

A key fits into a keyhole.
You must turn it to unlock
the door.

kick

When you kick you strike
out with your foot. Kick the
ball, not your brother!

kill

Kill is to make something
or someone die.

kilogram

In some countries, the
weight of something
is measured in kilograms.

kind

1. Kind means caring
towards others.
2. What kind of fruit
would you like?
This means what sort.

king

A king rules his country
or kingdom.

kitchen

You prepare and cook
food in the kitchen.
You wash-up there too!

kite

A kite is made up of
paper or cloth on a
wooden frame. It
flies high in the
sky lifted
by the
wind.

kitten

A young cat. Kittens
always love to play.

knife

A cutting utensil
with a sharp edge, used for
eating or as a weapon.

knee

This is the joint that makes
your leg bend, especially
when you kneel.

knight

Long ago knights wore
armor and fought
on horseback.

knit

When you knit
you make
clothes by
weaving
loops of wool
together on needles.

knob

A round lump on the
end or surface of
something. When you
open a door you turn
the knob.

knock

Knock at the door, but not too hard, or you will knock it down!

knot

When you tie a knot you join two pieces of string together.

Square knot

Fisherman's knot

Clove hitch

Half hitch

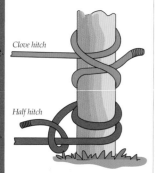

Sheet bend

know

Do you understand how to tie knots? Do you know how to do them? I knew you did!

L l

label

A label tells you about a thing or what is inside.

ladder

You climb up the rungs of a ladder to reach high places. Window cleaners always carry their ladders around.

lake

A large stretch of water with land all around.

lamp

There are many different kinds of lamps and they all give us light.

land

1. Land is the surface of the Earth that is not sea.
2. The airplane is about to land at the airport.

lane

A narrow road in the country. A narrow street in the town.

language

Words used by people to write and speak. There are many different languages.

large

Large is big, not little.

lasso

A cowboy uses a lasso for roping cattle. It is a long rope with a sliding loop.

last

1. Last means after all the others.
2. How long will this noise last? How long will it go on?

late

If you are late for school you arrive later than you should.

laugh

When people see something funny they laugh. Ha! Ha!

launch

When you launch a rocket into space or a ship into the sea, you start it moving.

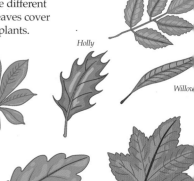

lawn

An area of grass in a garden. It is cut by a lawnmower to keep it short.

lay

1. Birds lay eggs. They produce them.
2. When we lay something down, we put it down carefully.

lazy

If you are lazy, you don't want to do any work.

lead

1. To lead is to show the way.
2. A dog has a lead. It is a strap that fits onto his collar.

learn

You learn if you find o facts or get to know how do things.

leave

When baby birds leav the nest they go away Leave them alone, the will be back next year

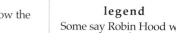

left

Left is opposite to righ

leg

Tables, chairs and peop are supported by legs

legend

Some say Robin Hood w a legend. Do you believe was real or just a story

leaf

Here are some different leaf shapes. Leaves cover trees and plants.

Horse chestnut

Ash

Holly

Willow

Oak

Sycamore

lemonade
[dr]ink made from lemons, water and sugar.

lend
[To] lend is to let a person [bo]rrow something for a little while.

length
[The] distance from one end to the other.

less
[Le]ss is not as much. I get [less] pocket money than Jim!

lesson
[A c]ertain length of time in which you learn.

letter
[Y]ou can write a message [t]o someone in a letter. [T]wenty-six letters make up the alphabet.

library
[A] place where collections [of b]ooks are kept. Borrow a [b]ook from your library!

lichen
[S]mall, flowerless plants that grow on plants and trees.

lid
[A l]id is a cover that closes a container.

lie
When you don't tell the truth, you lie. [W]hen you lie down, you remain flat.

life
[E]verything alive has life. Life is being alive.

lifeboat
A special boat full of brave men or women, who try to save people from drowning in the sea.

lift
To raise something up higher. Lift me up!

light
1. Things that are not heavy are light.
2. Light comes from the Sun and at night we must use lamps.

lighthouse
You will find a lighthouse near dangerous coasts. The winking light on top of the tower warns sailors of danger.

lightning
It flashes in the sky during a thunderstorm.

like
1. If you like a person, you are fond of them.
2. Like can mean almost the same.

line
Draw a line!

It can be straight or it can be curved.

lipstick
Make-up for your lips. Have I got too much lipstick on?

liquid
You can pour a liquid. It flows and is always wet.

listen
If you want to hear a sound, you must listen.

liter
A liter is a metric measurement used to measure liquids.

1 liter is about 1 ¹/₄ pints

little
Little means very small.

live
I live in a house, my fish lives in a bowl. I can't live in the water, he can't live out of it!

lobster
A shellfish with a tough shell and two very strong pincers.

lock
A lock fastens a door, a chest or a drawer. You must have the right key to unlock it.

long
How long is the pencil? How far is it from one end to the other?

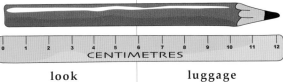

look
Look up, look down, look all around! You are using your eyes to see.

loose
If you have a loose tooth, it is not fixed. It wobbles!

lorry
A lorry is an English word for a truck that moves goods from place to place by road.

lose
When you lose something, although you search, you can't find it.

lot
What a lot of lettuces. I've never seen so many!

loud
You can hear a loud noise very easily.

love
To love someone is to like them as much as you can. I love my little baby sister so much. I want to cuddle her all the time!

luggage
When you go on vacation you take bags and cases full of clothes and other items that you will need. Lots of luggage!

lull
To soothe or calm. I will lull my baby to sleep with a gentle lullaby.

lumberjack
A man who cuts down trees ready for the mill.

lunch
A midday meal. It might be a quick snack or a great big bite!

M m

machine
Machines help us do our work easier and quicker. Here are a few that help us.

Lawn tractor

Hand mixer

Vacuum cleaner

Garden tiller

magic
No one can explain magic. Strange things happen when magic spells are cast!

magnet
Magnets are made of iron and steel. They attract or pull metal objects towards them.

magnify
Magnify is to make things bigger. Look under this magnifying glass.

make
If you make something you put it together. You make the dinner today!

male
Male is the opposite of female. Men and boys are male.

man
When a boy grows up he becomes a man.

many
Many means a lot. A Dalmatian has many spots.

map
A map is a drawing of a continent, a country or just a small area.

march
To march is to walk in step like soldiers.

margarine
This food is made from a blend of vegetable oils. You can spread it on bread or cook with it.

market
Lots of things are bought and sold from stalls in the farmer's market. Some markets are held outdoors.

marry
When a man and woman become husband and wife they marry.

mask
A mask covers your face. It can make you look very different.

match
1. You can light a match.
2. You can play in a match.
3. You can match things up.

meadow
A grass field full of wild flowers and plants.

meal
Breakfast, lunch, and dinner are meals.

measure
When we measure something, we find out the size of it or how much there is.

mechanic
A person who looks after engines.

medicine
If you are ill, medicine will help you get well.

meet
I am going to meet my friend! We are going to get together.

melt
The sun came out and my snowman turned to water. He melted!

mend
To mend is to repair something so it will be useful again.

mermaid
A legendary sea creatu with a woman's body a fish's tail for legs.

mess
If your room is a mess, very untidy.

message
When you send a mess you send words to ano person.

metal
Iron, steel, aluminiu copper and tin are a metals.

method
A method is a well thou out way to do somethi

meter
A meter is a metric measurement of length height.

microphone
It picks up sounds an makes them louder. Pick up the mike!

microscope
Tiny objects appear mu bigger under a microsc

midday
Midday is twelve noor

middle

middle is a point in the center, the same distance from either end.

midnight

Twelve o'clock at night, before a new day begins.

milk

We drink milk from cows and sometimes goats.

million

A thousand thousand.

miner

A man who works down a mine.

minus

minus means to subtract.

$$10 - 6 = 4$$

minute

Sixty seconds in a minute. Sixty minutes in one hour.

mirror

Look in the mirror! What do you see reflected in the glass?

miserable

When my parrot escaped, I felt very miserable.

miss

I miss my parrot so much. I wish he would come back!

---

2. I love to play goalie but I often miss the ball!

mist

Mist is like a fine rain or a light fog.

mistake

To make a mistake is to make an error.

mix

If you put different things together you mix them.

money

We use money when we buy things. We pay in coins and notes.

monster

A monster is a huge, horrible, frightening thing.

month

There are twelve months in a year.

JANUARY · FEBRUARY · MARCH
APRIL · MAY · JUNE · JULY
AUGUST · SEPTEMBER · OCTOBER
NOVEMBER · DECEMBER

moon

The Moon spins round the Earth. The Sun's light catches the Moon and makes it shine.

moonlight

When the Moon is full it shines with a silvery light called moonlight.

more

Mary has more apples than Ken. She has a greater amount.

morning

The morning comes after the night and goes on until midday.

---

most

Sara has the most flowers. She has the greater amount.

moth

Moths are not as colourful as butterflies. They fly at night.

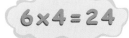

Tiger

Hawk

Emperor

mother

A mother is a woman who has had a child or children.

---

mug

You get more in a mug than a cup. What is your favorite drink – maybe a nice mug of hot chocolate?

mule

A cross between a horse and an ass.

multiply

You make something several times bigger if you multiply.

$$6 \times 4 = 24$$

muscle

Muscles are parts of the body that produce movement, they can only pull not push. We need two sets of muscles for each joint or limb, one to bend and one to straighten.

---

museum

A place where you can look at collections of interesting or historical things.

music

Different sounds made by instruments or a person's voice are music.

mystery

A mystery is something strange or puzzling that you cannot explain.

---

motorway

A modern fast road in England with three lanes in each direction. Similar to our freeways or interstates.

---

mountain

A gigantic hill with steep rocky sides. Some mountain peaks are covered in snow.

mouth

You use your mouth to speak and eat. Smile please!

move

Nothing stands still, even the Earth is moving all the time.

mud

Wet, sticky, soft earth is mud. Wipe your muddy boots!

N
n

nail

1. A thin piece of metal with a sharp point. You hammer it through two pieces of wood to join them together.

---

2. Nails are the hard parts on the tips of your fingers and toes.

name

Each person and every thing has a name. That is what they are called.

narrow

This opening is too narrow to squeeze through. It isn't wide enough!

N n

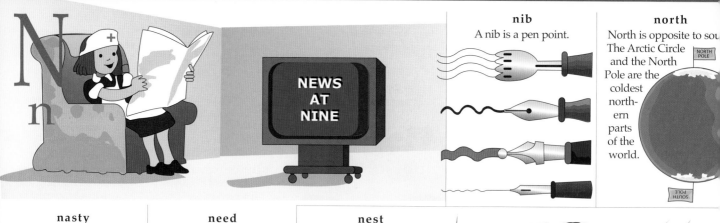

NEWS AT NINE

nib
A nib is a pen point.

north
North is opposite to sou... The Arctic Circle and the North Pole are the coldest northern parts of the world.

NORTH POLE
SOUTH POLE

nasty
How unpleasant. What a nasty black eye!

natural
Made by nature and not by man.

nature
The world around us, not changed by man in any way.

naughty
To behave badly in a mischievous way.

navy
The whole of a country's ships of war and all the sailors.

near
Near is close. I was so near to the shark I could have touched it!

nearly
He nearly fell in the river means he almost did.

nectar
Honey of flowers that bees collect.

neat
When you are neat you are tidy and put everything in the proper place.

need
When you need a thing it is necessary to have it. This gentleman needs a new suit!

needle
A thin pointed piece of metal with a slit at one end. Poke a thread through the slit and you can begin to sew.

neighbor
Someone who lives near by.

nervous
I am frightened of the shadows in my room. They make me very nervous.

nest
Most birds and a few animals make a nest for their young.

Coot

Stork

Woodpecker

Harvest mouse

Swallow

net
A net is for catching things without doing any damage.

never
Never is at no time, not ever. You will never be able to lift that!

nettle
A plant that stings if you touch it.

new
Something that has never been worn or has just been made. New is fresh, not old.

newspaper
Printed sheets of paper to read. They tell you the news every day.

next
You are next in line, so you can sit next to the driver. Next to means near, next means coming after.

nibble
Take little bites of something. Hamsters nibble their food.

nice
Nice means pleasant or kind. It can also mean dainty or accurate.

night
When the sun has set, it grows dark and night falls.

nobody
If a room is empty, there is nobody there!

noise
A sound of any kind. Susan was making too much noise in class, so the teacher told her off.

none
Paul had six bricks, Peter had none, not even one.

nonsense
Something silly.

noon
Noon is twelve o'clock midday.

nose
You breathe and smell through your nose.

not
You are not to throw th... Not is another way of saying no.

note
1. Mom wrote Dad a no... about his dinner.

2. When you play a tun... you hear and play lots... notes.

nothing
Nothing on your plate means not one thing.

notice
notice is a written sign for all to read.

2. Have you noticed Tom's arm? Have you seen it?

noun
noun is the name of a person, place or thing.

now
m going for a walk now. Now means at this very moment.

nowhere
hat is nowhere in sight. can't see it anywhere.

nuisance

nething that is annoying. hat bonfire is a nuisance.

number
symbol or word that says how many.

nurse
A person trained to look after the sick.

nursery
place where little children lay and are looked after.

nut
nut has a hard shell ith a kernel or ed inside.

Oo

oak
The oak is a great tree that grows from a tiny acorn.

oar
You row a boat with oars.

oasis
A fertile place in the desert with water and trees.

obey
The Genie of the Lamp obeyed Aladdin. He did as Aladdin told him.

occupation
What is this man's occupation? What job does he do?

ocean
An ocean is bigger than a sea.

o'clock
When we tell the time by the clock we say four o'clock.

octopus
A sea creature with eight arms or tentacles.

odd
1. An odd number cannot be divided by two like an even number.
2. Something strange or out of the ordinary. Sophie didn't wave to me today. That's odd.

off
Switch off the television! Jump off the chair! Off means not on.

offer
If you say you will do something, you offer to help. Mother offered to give Tom a ride.

office
People work in an office. It is their place of business.

officer
Someone who is in command and gives orders to people in the navy, army, airforce, the police or the fire department.

often
My dog often digs in the garden. He does it again and again.

ogre
A fairy-tale monster or man-eating giant.

oil
1. Oil is a greasy, black liquid that is found underground or under the sea bed.

Drilling for oil at sea

2. We use oil made from seeds and plants for cooking.

ointment
Put some ointment on your knees, they look sore!

old
An old person has lived a long time. An old thing has been used a lot and is no longer new.

only
James was the only one to win a rosette. No one else did, he was the only one.

open
Open means not shut. Alice went through the open door and opened her eyes wide.

opera
A musical play with singers instead of actors.

Horse chestnut   Almond   Peanut   Coconut

Brazil

Acorn   Hazelnut

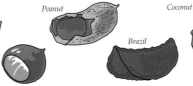

orchard

Fruit trees grow in an orchard.

orchestra

Many musicians playing together form an orchestra. Their instruments are in four different groups.

ordinary

Something ordinary has nothing special about it. What an ordinary house!

ornament

Ornaments are a decoration.

other

Here are two kittens, one is ginger, the other gray. One is different to the other.

our

Our ball has been stolen. It belonged to us.

out

We are going out to play. The sun is shining outside and we don't want to stay in.

outline

Draw an outline of your pet.

oval

Anything oval is shaped like an egg.

oven

You can roast and bake food in an oven.

over

1. The hen flew over the gate.
2. I am sad my vacation is over, or at an end.

overhead

The swans flew overhead. They passed above our heads.

overwhelm

To overwhelm is to crush or submerge. The noise in the football stadium was so overwhelming that Sandy left. It was just too much.

owe

If you owe money to someone then you have borrowed it and will have to pay it back.

owl

A bird of prey that flies at night.

own

If you own something it belongs to you. I own a puppy called Goldie.

ox

A bull or cow.

oxygen

Oxygen is one of the gases in air that all living things must have to live.

P p

pack

Father wants me to pack his shorts, but the case is packed to the brim.

paddle

Oh dear! My paddle is floating away.

page

A page is one side of a piece of paper in a book, magazine or newspaper.

pain

When you feel a pain it hurts. Your body is telling your brain something is wrong.

paint

If you paint a picture or a house, you are putting color on with a brush.

pair

A pair is two of the same thing. They go together.

palm

1. Dates and coconuts grow on palm trees. People use their leaves to thatch huts and make mats.

2. Hold out your hand, the inside or front is your palm.

pancake

Can you toss a pancake? A batter made of eggs, flour and milk is poured into a frying-pan and cooked into a pancake.

paper

Paper is made from pulped up wood, which is pressed and rolled into sheets.

parachute

When you jump out of a plane your parachute opens like an umbrella, and you float safely downwards.

parcel

Something wrapped i paper and fastened wi string or tape.

parents

Mothers and fathers a parents.

park

1. An open space with grass and trees that everyone can use.
2. Have I parked my ca in the wrong place?

party

A party is a group of people. When people celebrate they love a par

pass

1. That motorbike is goi to pass us.
2. I have lost my bus pa
3. The cowboy rode thro the mountain pass.
4. My aunt has pass her driving test at last.
5. Pass the ketchup please!

passenger

A person who travels i a plane, boat, train or motor vehicle.

PASSENGERS ONLY

passport

You need your passport to travel from one country to another.

past

Something that happened in the past, usually means it happened long ago.

pastry

When you rub fat into flour and roll it out with a rolling pin, you have made pastry dough.

pat

When you pat your dog you tap him gently to show you are pleased with him.

pattern

Do you like to draw or paint a pattern?
2. A dress pattern has shapes that fit together on material. Cut out and sewn together, they make a dress.

paw

Animals have paws. Who made these paw marks?

Dog

Fox

Badger

Rabbit

Cat

Mouse

pay

When you buy something, you must pay for it with money.

peace

Peace means no fighting or war. It can also mean quiet and calm. How peaceful!

peanut

Peanuts grow underground. Have you tasted roasted peanuts and peanut butter?

PEANUT BUTTER

pearl

If you are lucky you may find a pearl in an oyster. You need lots of pearls to make a necklace.

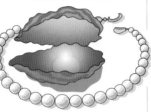

pebble

Little smooth stones found on beaches or river-beds.

pedal

When you pedal your bicycle with your feet on the pedals, you make the wheels move.

peel

The peel is the skin of fruit and vegetables. This apple has been peeled.

pen

You use a pen for writing with ink.

pencil

A pencil is a wooden stick with a thin lead through the middle.

HB

penguin

A flightless bird that lives in arctic conditions.

peninsula

A bit of land that is almost surrounded by water.

penknife

A knife small enough to keep in your pocket. It has blades that fit into the handle. Also called a pocketknife.

people

Men, women and children are all people.

perfect

When a thing is perfect, it has no faults at all. Your sewing is perfect!

perform

If you perform something, you carry it out or do it. What a performance!

perfume

A sweet smelling scent from flowers or in a bottle.

person

Every single man, woman and child is a person. Animals are not.

pet

An animal kept at home in your house or yard.

phobia

A fear of something. Many people have a phobia of spiders.

photograph

A picture taken with a camera. Do you like having your photo taken?

piano

When you play the piano and your fingers press the keys, lots of tiny hammers hit wires and make the different notes.

pick

1. If you pick flowers you collect or gather them up.

2. Pick a card! You can choose any one.

picnic

A packed meal eaten out of doors.

picture

A picture is a drawing or a painting. It can also be a photograph.

pie

Something good to eat inside a pastry crust.

piece

If you take a piece of pie, you take part of it.

pile

Things heaped up on top of each other are in a pile.

pill

A pill is medicine made into a little ball or easy-to-swallow shape.

pillar

Posts that hold up porches, arches and buildings.

pillow

A soft cushion on a bed.

pilot

A pilot steers an airplane.

pin

Shaped like a small needle with a tiny round head at one end.

pipe

1. Does your grandpa smoke a pipe?

2. Pipes can carry liquid or gas. They are hollow tubes.

place

This is my place at the table! It is your special spot where you are.

plan
1. A plan is a drawing of an object or a building from above.
2. Those naughty boys have a plan. Have you any idea what it is?

platform
1. A raised floor like a small stage.
2. I sat on the platform waiting for the train.

play
1. A play is a story which is acted out in front of an audience.

2. When you play, forget work and have fun!
3. You play a musical instrument. Harry can play the xylophone very well.

plow
A tractor or horse pulls a plow as it cuts and turns the soil.

plug
A thing that fits into a hole.

plunge
Sam plunged into the water.

poor
If you are poor you ha very little money o possessions.

population
The number of people live in one particular pl

porridge
Do you eat porridge your breakfast?

polite
If you have good manners and behave well, people will say you are polite.

pollute
To make the Earth dirty and dangerous by getting rid of trash carelessly.

pond
A pool of water full of interesting wildlife in the water or around its edge.

possible
If a thing is possible it can be done.

poster
Someone has stu posters all ove this wall.

postman
A person who collects and deli letters and packa

pour
You pour liquid out o one container into something else.

powder
Powder is like dust, ve fine and light.

powerful
Powerful means very strong. That engine loc really powerful.

praise
When you praise a pers you tell them they hav done well. Congratulatic

prepare
The chef prepared the pi He got it ready.

planet
There are nine major planets that spin round the Sun. The Earth is one.

 Jupiter
 Uranus
Pluto
Neptune

Mars
Earth
Mercury
Venus
Sun
Saturn

plant
A plant is a living thing which usually grows in soil. It also needs water, air and sunlight.

playground
A place for children to enjoy themselves. It is usually outdoors and might have swings, a slide or a jungle gym.

please
1. Ask nicely - if you say "please" politely then you can have another ride on my bicycle!
2. My aunt is very pleased with me. I have made her happy.

plus
Two plus two equals four. Plus means to add to.

poem
A poem describes something, usually in rhyme. Can you write poetry?

point
1. The sharp end of a thing.
2. It's very rude to point.

poison
A harmful or fatal substance.

police
People who are trained to keep law and order.

plastic
A man-made material which can be pressed and molded into many shapes.

Water boatman
Great diving beetle
Tadpole
Smooth newt
Great pond snail

present
A present is a gift to give or to receive.

pretend
When you pretend, you make-believe. Lucy is pretending she is grown-up.

pretty
Doesn't this little girl look pretty. She thinks she does too!

price
What is the price of that on? How much money do I need to buy it?

prince
son of a king or queen.

princess
daughter of a king or queen.

print
print is an impression or k, like a fingerprint or footprint.

printing
ing words and pictures book or newspaper is on a printing machine. ters covered in ink are essed or printed onto paper.

prize
reward for winning. his little pig has won first prize.

problems
roblems are always difficult to solve.

program
What is your favorite ogram on television? Paul collects football game programs.

promise
To give your word and keep it. Dad promised we could go to the zoo.

protect
All animals and birds protect their young. They shield them from danger and harm.

proud
Mother was very proud when Dad won the race.

prove
To prove is to show something can be done or that it is true.

pudding
A pudding is the sweet tasting dessert.

puddle
A small pool of water outside in the road or inside on the floor.

pull
The tug-of-war team pulled hard on the rope. Each side is trying to make the rope come towards them.

pump
When your tires are flat, you use a pump to force air into them.

punch
To punch is to hit hard with your fists. Boxers punch with their gloves on.

pupil
Here are some pupils from Dinglewood School learning their lessons!

puppet
Puppets are dolls that move if somebody else pulls the strings.

purse
A purse is a small bag to keep your money safe.

push
When you push, you press against something until it moves.

puzzle
A puzzle is difficult to solve or understand.

Qq

quack
When ducks make a noise, they quack.

quarrel
If you quarrel with someone, you get angry and argue.

quarter
Cut a thing into four equal parts and you have four quarters. One of the parts is a quarter.

queen
A woman who rules a country or the wife of a king.

question
You ask a question to find out something. What is on the blackboard? The answer to that question is, a question mark!

quick
Quick means fast or speedy. Be quick! Then you will win the race.

quiet
To be quiet is to be silent and make no noise at all.

quilt
A padded cover for a bed. Here is a patch-work quilt.

quiz
A quiz is like a test, but shorter. You must answer a number of questions.

R r

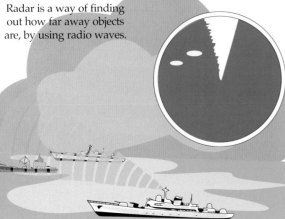

reply
To reply is to answe[r]
"Who are you?" ask[ed]
Alice. "The White Rab[bit,"]
he replied.

reporter
A reporter interviewe[d]
today. Perhaps we w[ill]
be on television or in [the]
newspapers tomorro[w.]

reptile
A cold blooded creat[ure]
with a scaly skin.

Lizard

Tortoise

Croc[odile]

radar
Radar is a way of finding
out how far away objects
are, by using radio waves.

recipe
A recipe
tells you
how to
make a
dish and
what to
put in it.

Strawberry Mousse
11b Strawberries
3 Eggs
4oz Sugar
10oz Cream
1 tsp Gelatine

recite
When you recite a poem,
you say it out loud.

record
This pole-vaulter has just
set a new world record.

remain
Father remained to fix
the leak. He stayed
behind and we left!

remember
To keep something in
your mind and not
forget. Remember the
steep hill!

Sna[ke]

rescue
If you save a person f[rom]
danger you rescue the[m.]

raft
A raft is a floating boat,
sometimes made of logs
lashed together.

rain
When it rains, water drops
from clouds in the sky and
falls down to Earth.

rainbow
Rainbows are caused by
sunlight shining through
raindrops. A rainbow is split
up into seven colors.

rare
Something rare is
uncommon. There are not
many of them.

raw
Raw meat and vegetables
are not cooked.

ray
Rays from a lamp are beams
of light. Sunbeams are thin
rays of sunlight.

razor
Father shaves with a razor.
It has a very sharp blade.

reach
1. To reach is to stretch
towards something.
2. We have reached the sea
at last. We have got there.

read
You look at words and
understand them.

ready
Are you ready to go
camping? Are you prepared
with all you need?

real
This is not a real man, it's a
toy. The little boy is just
pretending he's real.

receive
To receive something
is to be given it.

referee
A referee makes sure the
players keep to the rules of
the game.

refrigerator
An ice-cold cupboard that
keeps food fresh and cool.

remind
When you remind someone
you jog their memory.
Did you remember to
water my plant?

remove
Remove your muddy shoes.
Take them off!

repair
Broken things must be
repaired.

rest
1. When you feel tire[d]
sit down and rest.
2. Leave the washing-[up.]
I will do the rest of it [later.]

restaurant
Meals are served in [a]
restaurant. You get a [bill]
when you have finish[ed.]

return
1. When John returne[d the]
model, it was broke[n.]
2. Swallows come [to]
England in March a[nd]
return to Africa in
September.

reward
...ward is like a prize. You ...ight get a reward for finding something.

rhyme
...rds sounding the same. ...hymes are small poems ...ke nursery rhymes.

rhythm
...e a tambourine in time ...the music and you've got rhythm.

rice
...e is a grain like grass. ...grows in ...flooded ...h water.

ride
...be carried along by a ...achine or an animal.

right
...ight is opposite to left. ...m I right in thinking ...come from Australia?

ring
...ring fits your finger. A ring can be a circle shape. ...ells ring ding-a-dong!

rink
...very large area with ...enty of room for ice-...ting or roller skating.

ripe
...When fruit is ripe, it is ready to eat.

rise
...t up in the morning, ...nd shine. The sun has risen in the sky.

roar
...hen lions and tigers ...ke a noise, they roar.

river
Rivers begin in the hills as small streams. They grow deeper and wider then flow into the sea.

road
A road is a way on which people and vehicles travel.

rob
To rob is to steal. There's been a robbery at the bank, and the robber is getting away!

robot
A mechanical man. Andrew has a toy robot.

rock
1. Rock the baby's cradle from side to side.
2. A rock is a large stone. Rock climbing can be dangerous.

rocket
1. A firework on a stick.
2. Astronauts travel through space in a rocket.

roll
The wheel went rolling down the hill, it turned over and over.

roof
The roof covers the top of a building.

room
Rooms are different parts of a building or house.

root
Dig up a plant, growing beneath the soil are the roots.

rope
A long thick twisted cord made up of lots of thin cords.

rough
1. The sea looks rough today.
2. What a rough hand you have, Mr. Gorilla.

round
A circle has a round shape and so has a ball.

row
1. These flowers are in a row.

2. Row a boat on the lake.

rub
To move and press one thing hard against another. Rub your hands.

rubber
Rubber comes from the sap of a tree. Lots of things are made from it.

rubbish
Throw out all that rubbish! You don't need that trash any more.

rule
Orders that must be obeyed.

ruler
1. A ruler is a person who governs a country.
2. Used to measure things.

run
Here are some runners running a race. How fast can you run?

rung
Climb up the ladder rung by rung.

S s

sad
Sally is sad, she is feeling very unhappy about something.

saddle
A seat on a bicycle or a horse.

safe
Now he is safe, he is not in any danger.

sail
When the wind fills the sails the boat sails along. These sailors have sailed many a sea.

salad
Traditionally, vegetables or fruit eaten without cooking, although there are many fancy variations.

same
These twins look the same. They are alike except for the smudge on Gary's nose.

S s

sand
Grains of sand are made by rocks and shells ground down by the weather and the sea.

sandal
An open shoe with straps.

sandwich
To make a sandwich you put your favorite food between two slices of bread.

sauce
Sauces add flavor to food.

save
1. When you save money you keep it to use later.
2. If you are a lifeguard you are trained to save lives.

scales
1. A weighing machine.
2. The hard flakes on the skin of fish and snakes.
3. Musical exercises.

school
Students go to school to learn. At the beginning they are taught to read and write.

science
In science we learn things by experiments, study and careful testing.

scissors
Scissors have two sharp blades fixed in the middle. They can cut paper, cloth and even your hair.

scooter
I can go really fast on my scooter!

scream
My mouse escaped and made my sister scream.

screw
A screw is like a nail with grooves, which fastens wood together. You use a screwdriver to turn a screw.

scroll
1. A roll of parchment or paper.
2. An ornamental shape

sculptor
A sculptor carves objects in stone and wood. They are called sculptures.

sea
Sea is salt water that covers a great part of our Earth.

search
When I searched for my tie, I looked everywhere.

season
There are four seasons, each one is a quarter of a year.

seaweed
Plants that grow in the sea.

secret
Something only one person knows, until they tell somebody else.

see
I can see you! Can you see me?

seed
New plants grow from the seeds of the old plants.

sell
The super-market sells fruit. They sold me a pineapple.

seesaw
One side goes up, as the other side goes down.

self
When I'm by myself, I'm all alone. Myself is me.

send
Send Tim to fetch the ball. Make him go and get it.

sentence
I broke my leg and had to walk on crutches. That sentence tells you in a few words a complete happening.

sentry
A soldier on guard. This soldier has a sentry box.

several
Several is more than one, perhaps two or three.

sew
A needle and thread and a piece of cloth is all you need to sew.

shadow
When the sun is shining, your shadow goes everywhere with you.

shake
To shake something you move it up and down or from side to side.

shallow
Shallow water is not deep.

shampoo
I get shampoo in my eyes every time Dad washes my hair!

shape
Everything and everybody has a different shape.

share
When I shared my gra with Kim, I gave her of them.

sharp
Don't play with kniv They are sharp and ca you.

shed
A little hut outdoor for storing tools and kinds of things.

sheet
1. Mother has the bed s hanging on the clothes
2. Writing letters can sheets and sheets of pa

shelf
The shelf in my room full, so my Dad put up more shelves.

shell
Eggs and nuts have a shell covering. So do s animals and sea creatur protect themselves

shelter
You can find shelter u my umbrella, it will pr you from the rain!

shine
1. If the sun shines it g out a bright light.
2. When I have polishe shoes, they really shi

ship

...large boat which can cross oceans.

shop

...erent shops sell different ...gs. What will you buy today?

short

...t is neither tall nor long. ...Which is the shortest pencil?

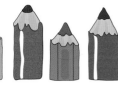

shorts

...oing sports we all wear shorts!

shout

...ple shout ...en they ...nt to be ...ard.

...ower

...shower ...quick sprinkling of rain. ...aking a shower on a hot ...ay is very refreshing.

shrink

...you have a shower in ...ur suit, it will shrink.

shut

...When a thing is shut, ...t is closed; not open.

sick

...don't feel well today. I feel sick.

sign

...ign is a notice that tells ...ou something.

silent

...o be silent is ...keep quiet.

silk

...fine thread ...spun by ...lkworms ...d woven ...nto cloth.

silver

A precious metal that shines when polished.

similar

This book is similar to the other. It is almost the same.

simple

This game is simple, not difficult at all.

sing

You make music with your voice when you sing a song.

sink

1. The kitchen sink is full of dishes.

2. If your boat has a hole it will sink.

size

How big or how small you are is your size.

skeleton

All the bones in your body fit together and form your skeleton.

ski

Here is a skier skiing down a ski slope.

skin

Humans and animals have skin covering their body. Fruit and vegetables have skin too.

sky

The sky is up above you. It can be blue in the day, black at night, and sometimes grey and cloudy.

skyscraper

Skyscrapers are such high buildings, they seem to touch the sky.

sleep

Animals, birds and people, go to sleep to rest.

slice

To slice is to cut into flat thin pieces.

slow

Slugs and snails can't speed along, they always go slow!

small

Small is little; not big or tall.

smell

Some things smell lovely, some things smell terrible. Your nose tells you.

smile

You smile and look happy when you are pleased.

smoke

As a fire burns it gives off smoke.

smooth

A smooth thing has no bumps or sharp points.

sneeze

When something tickles our nose, like pollen or dust, we sneeze.

snow

Tiny crystals of ice which form snowflakes then fall from the sky as snow.

soap

A good wash with soap and water makes the dirt disappear.

soft

Fur and feathers are soft to the touch, not hard at all.

soil

Plant a seed in the soil and watch it grow.

soldier

A soldier is a man in the army. These are soldiers from the past.

U.S. 1812

English 1815

German 1812

English 1814

Belgian 1789

solve

To solve a puzzle or a mystery is to find the answer.

something

You never say what "something" actually is. I have something to show you!

sometime

At some time in the past or future.

sometimes

Occasionally. Sometimes we have a treat after our meal.

son

A son is the boy child of a mother and father.

song

A song is like a poem or rhyme set to music.

soon

I will go to bed soon, in a little while.

sorry

1. I felt sorry that the blackbird died. It made me feel sad.

2. Sorry I broke your vase. I do apologize.

sound

Every noise you hear is a sound.

soup

Soup is a liquid food with lots of flavor, made from meat and vegetables.

sour

Some citrus fruits like lemons and limes taste sour.

south

South is the point opposite to north. Countries with the word south in their name are usually hot.

space

A space is a place with nothing in it. There is no picture below, just a space.

speak

When you speak on the telephone you say something to the person at the other end.

special

Something special is not ordinary but different.

speed
Christmas is a special time.
Speed is the rate you travel. High speed or low speed.

spell
1. Witches love casting evil spells.
2. To put the letters of a word in the right order.

spend
1. How much money will I have to spend to buy that?
2. I spend a lot of time at my Grandmother's house.

spill
When you knock over some liquid you spill it.

spin
1. A top spins when it turns round and round.
2. Spin on a spinning wheel and make a thread.
3. A spider spins to make a web.

splash
Jump into a pool. You will hear the splash as the water splashes out.

spot
A spot is a little mark. Spots are lots of little marks.

spread
When the baker spreads icing on a cake, he covers the top evenly.

spring
The first season of the year. Winter has passed and things start to grow.

square
A square has four corners and four straight sides of the same length.

squeeze
When you squeeze a lemon, you crush it or press it hard.

squint
To narrow your eyes so you can see when it is bright outside. It is so sunny outside that you may have to squint your eyes if you forgot your sunglasses.

stable
A building where horses are kept.

stairs
Steps for walking up and down to different levels of a building.

stamp
1. Stick a stamp on an envelope, then a rubber stamp will stamp the letter.

2. Do you ever stamp your foot when you're angry?

stand
Stand up, get on your feet! Don't sit there all day!

star
You can see stars at night as twinkling points of light in the dark sky. They are objects in space millions of miles away.

start
To start a thing is to begin it. Start the race!

station
Travelers on trains and buses arrive and depart at the station.

stationary
When a vehicle or person has stopped and is no longer moving.

stationery
Writing paper, pens, pencils, erasers are all stationery, sold at the store.

stay
Stay where you are. Don't move from that spot!

steal
To steal is to take things that don't belong to you. The magpie stole the necklace!

steam
When water boils it turns into a misty cloud called steam.

steep
A hillside that is steep, slopes sharply.

step
Walk forward, back, and to the side, you are taking steps.

stick
1. Chop the logs into sticks.
2. Stick the paper on the wall.

sting
Bees and wasps can sting you with their tails.

stir
If you stir something with a spoon, you mix it up and move it round.

stitch
Push a needle and thread in and out of cloth and you have stitches.

stop
To stop is to cease wh you are doing.

store
Animals store food for winter. It is kept in a sa place until it is neede

storm
Thunder, lightning, wi and rain all add up to storm.

story
Tell a story about Alad Is it true or made up

straight
Draw a straight line with a ruler.

stranger
A stranger is someone y don't know. Don't talk strangers!

stream
A little river of fresh running water.

street
A road with houses ar shops on both sides.

stretch
If you stretch a thing it g longer or wider. When y stretch you reach out.

stretcher
He was carried to hospital o stretch

sport
Sport is a game or pastime.

Golf

Football

Cricket

Soccer

Tennis

Baseball

Basketball

stripe
...pes are lines of different colors.

strong
Strong is powerful. ...ook at this strong man lifting weights.

sum
When you add two or more numbers together, the total is the sum.

summer
The warmest season of the year. We hope it is hot on our summer vacation.

sun
The Sun gives us light and heat although it is about 93 million miles away.

sunburn
If we stay too long in the hot sun we go red and get painful sunburns.

supermarket
A huge store full of all kinds of food and other goods to buy.

surface
The top or outside of something.

surname
Your surname is your last name.

surprise
If you don't expect something to happen, it comes as a surprise. Have you ever been to a surprise party?

surrender
The soldiers knew that they had to surrender because the enemy was far too powerful.

survive
To endure or live through something difficult. You cannot survive in the desert without water.

sweet
1. A dessert at the end of a meal.
2. This bag of candy taste sweet.
3. This kitten looks so sweet.

swim
Everybody ought to learn to swim to be safe in the water.

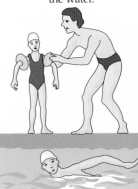

submarine
...oat that can sail on top ...f the water, then dive ...erneath and stay there.

A submarine rises to the surface by pumping air into the ballast tanks down each side.

To sink beneath the surface again the tanks are flooded with sea water

subtract
...btract is to take away.

$2 - 5 = 7$

sudden
...f a sudden an owl flew ...of the tree. It happened unexpectedly.

sugar
...ar makes things sweet. ...omes from sugar cane and sugar beets.

suit
...s that your new suit? ...pants are too short and ...e jacket is too long!

supper
An evening meal.

sure
I am sure my invitation said come in fancy dress. I am quite certain!

surf
Huge waves that crash onto the shore. Dare you ride the surf on a surfboard?

Tt

table
A piece of furniture with four legs and a flat top.

tadpole
A tiny, black creature that wriggles out of frog-spawn, grows quickly and becomes a frog.

tail
A tail is the piece at the end. Animals' tails are at the end of their bodies.

take
When you take something you hold it with your hands. Sometimes you take things from one place to another, like taking the dog for a walk.

tall
Tall is high. A giraffe is tall but the trees are taller.

tame
Some animals are friendly and happy with people. They are tame not wild.

tap
To knock gently is to tap.

tape recorder
A machine that can record sound on tape and play it back.

taste
We taste with our tongue, bitter, sweet or sour. When you eat a thing you taste it.

teacher
A teacher helps you to understand about many things. My teacher is teaching me all about Egypt.

team
A team is a group of people or animals working or playing together.

telephone
You can speak to someone far away on a telephone. Your voice is carried along wires to another phone.

Telephone exchange

telescope

When you look through a telescope you can see a long way, the lens makes things look bigger and nearer.

television

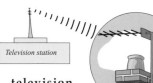

A television gives us pictures and sounds from signals sent through the air a long distance away. We need a digital antenna or a cable to receive them.

theater

You go to see a play or movie in a theater.

there

"There" is somewhere else, it is not here. The balloon is over there. There it goes towards the mountain!

through

Through means from one side to the other. The builder knocked a hole through our wall!

throw

When you throw something you make it move through the air away from you.

ticket

A ticket shows how much you paid for something or to go somewhere.

tie

1. A tie is fastened round the neck in a knot or bow.
2. To tie a thing is to fasten it securely.

tight

This man's shirt is too tight. His buttons are popping off. It fits him too closely.

timber

Timber is wood which has been cut into pieces ready to use in building.

time

Time measures how long things take. What time did you leave school? Is it time to go yet?

tired

I'm so tired, I need a rest!

toboggan

A sledge turned up at the front for sliding down snowy slopes.

today

Today is this very day. It's Fred's birthday today!

together

Lucy and her cat play together every day. They are with each other all the time.

tomorrow

It is Saturday today. Tomorrow will be Sunday.

tonight

1. Tonight is the night after this day.
2. Mom is getting ready to go out tonight.

tool

There are lots of different tools that help us do our work.

tooth

This baby has one tooth, soon he will have many more. You use your teeth to bite and chew. Take care of them with a toothbrush and toothpaste.

top

The highest point of anything is the top.

torch

Fire on the end of a stick used long ago to provide light.

touch

To touch is to feel with your hand. Wet paint, don't touch!

tough

Tough things are har and don't break easi My sister's rock cake are tough!

towel

A soft, thick cloth for dr pots and people.

tower

A tall, high, narrow building or just part of

town

A town is full of peop streets, shops and hou It is not as big as a ci

tractor

A tractor pulls farm machine and mo heav lo

traffic

All vehicles that move traffic, along the roads in the air.

traffic lights

These lights control moving traffic at busy junctions and crossroad

train

An engine pulling ca on a track.

trampoline

Jump on the trampoline how high you can spri

tell

"I must tell you what happened to me." Then Joe told us all about his accident.

temperature

How hot or cold something is. The instrument that measures temperature is a thermometer.

tent

A shelter you can fold up and take anywhere.

terrible

Last night there was a terrible fire. It was horrible and very frightening.

test

1. We are having a math test to find out how much we know.
2. The man tested the hose and found it was working.

thank

If you are grateful for some-thing, you say thank you.

thick

Wear a thick coat as the snow is very thick on the ground.

thin

Thin is opposite to thick. The oak tree trunk is thick, the silver birch is thin.

think

When you think, you are using your brains. Think about this problem.

thirsty

To be thirsty is to want a drink. Little children always feel thirsty in the middle of the night!

thousand

Ten hundreds are one thousand.

transparent
[Yo]u can see right through [thi]ngs that are transparent.

trap
[I]f an animal is caught [in] a trap it can't escape.

trapeze
[Lo]ok at the girl swinging high up on the trapeze.

travel
[To] travel is to go from one place to another.

treasure
[I] think they have found buried treasure.

tree
[T]ree lives longer than any [ot]her plant. It has a trunk, [with] branches and leaves.

triangle
A shape with three sides joined.

trick
[Can] a magician really [s]aw a lady in half, or is it a trick?

trouble
[I]f you upset a person or [m]ake things difficult, you are causing trouble.

truck
A truck is a large vehicle for carrying goods.

true
Something that is true is certain and not a lie.
Is it true that chameleons change color?

try
Try to climb to the top.
Do your best and try hard!

t-shirt
A shirt with short sleeves shaped like a T.

tunnel
When a train goes into a tunnel it travels through a long dark passage cut through the ground.

turn
If something turns it goes round. Watch me turn the wheel!

typewriter
This office machine has lots of keys with a letter on each one. When they are pressed they print words on paper.

tire
When the tires of your bicycle are full of air, they help you ride along smoothly.

twin
A twin is one of two children born at the same time to one mother. Animals often have twins too.

U u

ugly
Cinderella's sisters were not pretty, they were Ugly Sisters.

umbrella
We open our umbrella to shield us from the rain, then close it when the rain stops.

uncle
The brother of your mother or father is your uncle.

under
Under means below.
What are you doing under the table?

understand
If you understand something you know what it means.

underwear
The clothes worn next to your skin.

undress
To take off your clothes.

unhappy
This little girl looks unhappy. I wonder why?

unicorn
A fairy tale animal with the body of a horse and a horn on its head.

uniform
Uniforms are the clothes of the same kind of people in a job or school.

Fireman

Nurse

Policeman

Post lady

unique
One of a kind, different from every other one. Each one of us is unique!

unite
We are united in our fight to save the whales from extinction. We are joined together as one.

unkind
The other birds were unkind to the Ugly Duckling. They were cruel and hurt his feelings.

untidy
Messy. Do you think this little boy is untidy?

up
To go up is to rise. Up is the opposite of down.

upside-down
When you are upside-down, you are the wrong way up.

upstairs
Jane is climbing the stairs to bed. Her room is upstairs.

urgent
These medicines are very urgent. A patient needs them at once!

useful
Useful things are helpful.
The red bucket is useful, just right for the job.

useless
Useless things are of no use at all. The blue bucket is quite useless because it is broken.

V v

view
This artist is painting the view. He is painting the landscape as far as he can see.

vitamins
Vitamins help to make y[...] body strong and healt[...] They are found in ma[...] foods.

vacant
This house is vacant. It is empty with nothing and nobody inside.

valley
The lower ground that lies between two hills.

vehicle
Anything that carries goods or people from place to place. Cars, trucks, buses, even wagons and bicycles are all vehicles.

vein
Blood returns to the heart for more oxygen through the veins in your body.

vet
Vet is short for veterinarian. A person who cares for sick animals.

viaduct
A road or railway bridge over a valley.

victory
When people or teams compete, one must lose and the other wins the victory.

village
A village is much smaller than a town. It is in the country surrounded by farmland.

villain
A wicked person. We almost always have a villain and a hero in a story.

voice
You open your mouth a[...] use your voice to spea[...]

volcano
A mountain that throws red-hot lava, ash and ga[...] through a hole in the to[...]

vanish
When things vanish, they disappear without a trace.

varnish
A paint which has a glossy finish.

vase
You put flowers in a vase. Make sure they have some water.

verb
Verbs tell of something being done. Swing, jump, laugh, play, are all verbs.

verse
"There was a bee sat on a wall. It said buzz and that was all!"

video recorder
A machine that records sounds and pictures on tape, then plays them back through your television.

The TV signal is picked up by the antenna on the roof. It then goes into the video recorder where it can be recorded. And then onto the TV where you can see the picture.

video tape
A special tape for recording sounds and pictures in a video recorder.

vegetable
A plant grown for food that is not a fruit.

Cabbage
Cucumber
Turnip
Tomato
Carrot
Potato
Onion
Lettuce
Mushroom
Beans
Peas
Corn

violin
A musical instrument with four strings played with a bow.

visit
When someone calls to see you they pay you a visit. They are visitors.

vow
A solemn promise. Marriage vows are prom[...] that a bride and groom make to one another.

vowels
The letters a, e, i, o, u are vowels.

voyage
A long journey far acros[...] the sea.

W
w

wheelbarrow
A little cart with one wheel in front and two handles and legs behind.

wagon
…arts or trucks that can …rry heavy loads from …lace to place by road or rail.

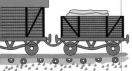

waist
…ou wear a belt round your waist.

walk
…use our legs and feet to …lk. We move along by …ting one foot in front of the other.

wall
A boundary made of …icks or stones, also the …side of a house.

want
…his little girl wants her …ther. She needs her and …ishes she would come.

warm
…Warm is between hot …d cold. It's cold outside. …me and warm yourself by the fire!

warn
…someone is in danger …d you tell them about it, you warn them.

wash
When we are dirty, water washes us clean. Most things come clean with water.

washing machine
A machine for washing lots of dirty clothes in a short time.

watch
1. You wear a watch on your wrist to tell you the time.
2. This boy is going to watch the game. He loves looking at football.

water
All living things need water to live. Water falls to Earth as rain, filling rivers, lakes and oceans.

watering can
We need water to drink and so do plants. When it is dry, water the flowers with a watering can.

wave
1. The President waved to me as he went by, and I waved my flag.
2. The surface of the sea moves up and down in waves.

way
1. How you do something is the way you do it. This is the way to stand on your head!
2. Do you know the way to the Moon?

wear
You wear clothes on your body. Dad is wearing his gardening clothes. The knees are worn out.

weather
Everybody talks about the weather. Is it wet or dry today? Will it rain, snow or blow?

weed
Gardeners think weeds are a nuisance, they pull them up because they are wild plants that they don't want in their garden.

week
A week has seven days. There are fifty-two weeks in a year.

weigh
If you weigh something you find out how heavy it is. How much do you weigh?

wheel
A wheel is a round shape that turns on its axle or center. Wheels help things move more easily.

when
When will the train come? I will put your luggage aboard when you get on!

where
Where is my tie? It is where you left it.

which
Which asks what thing out of two or more things. Which watch has the second hand?

whisker
What a fine set of whiskers!

whisper
A whisper is a soft little voice. Whisper in my ear!

who
Who did that? Who threw that? Who broke that? "Who" asks "whatever" person.

whole
Something that is whole is all there, nothing is missing. Mark said he could eat a whole French loaf!

why
"Why are you dressed like that?" When someone asks why, they want to know the reason.

"I am going to play football!"

wide
This river is wide, it is broad not narrow.

wig
Artificial hair for the head.

wigwam
Indians lived in tents called wigwams. They are made from poles covered in animal skins or tree bark.

wild
Animals that are wild are not tame. Wild plants grow in fields not in a garden.

wind
The wind is air that is moving. Some winds are just a gentle breeze. See what a strong wind can do!

wind
To wind is to turn and twist. You wind up the clock by turning the key. Here is a road winding up a steep mountain side.

windmill
A mill that is driven by the force of the wind pushing the sails round. Windmills are used for grinding corn or pumping water.

window
A window in a building is made of glass to let in light. It can be opened to let in fresh air.

windshield
A transparent shield in a vehicle to stop the wind and rain from getting inside. It protects the passengers.

wing
Birds, insects and planes need wings to help them fly.

winter
The coldest season. Nights are long and dark and the days are short and cold with frost and snow.

wire
Wire is a thread made of metal. Different wires carry electricity and telephone signals to our houses.

wish
Make a wish! You really would like that wish to come true.

witch
Witches cast magic spells, but only in fairy tales!

wizard
A wizard is a man from legends and stories who can use magic.

woman
When a girl grows up she becomes a woman.

wood
1. A small group of trees, not as big as a forest, is called a wood.
2. Wood is a material that comes from trees. It is used in buildings and furniture and many other ways.

wool
The wool from sheep is spun into yarn then woven into cloth. Woollen clothes are warm and soft.

work
When anyone works they do a job. What work does this woman do?

world
Everything around us is our world. The Earth and sky is the world in which we live.

wrap
When it is cold mothers wrap up their babies tightly in covers before they go out.

write
When you write you put down words. You could write a few words, a letter, a story or a whole book.

wrong
Something wrong is not right or correct. Sarah has the wrong answer.

x-ray
Have you ever had a broken bone x-rayed? Invisible x-rays from a camera can pass through your flesh and take photographs which show doctors the inside of your body.

xylophone
A musical instrument made of pieces of wood or metal, each making a different note when hit by a hammer held in either hand.

yacht
A yacht travels fast when the wind fills its sails.

yard
Yards are areas of hard ground outside houses and schools.

yawn
When you are tired or bored, you open your mouth wide and yawn.

year
This baby is one-year-old. She has lived 12 months or 52 weeks or 365 days.

yesterday
If today is Sunday, yesterday was Saturday.

yoga
My sister is practicing her yoga. She is doing exercises and thinking.

yogurt
A food made from mi which tastes thick an creamy. Which flavor you like?

yolk
The yellow part of an e

young
When you are young, y are not grown-up. Every was young once!

your
Something that is you belongs to you. I know is your notebook. It ha your name all over it

youth
1. A young person.
2. The time when you are young.

zebra
A zebra is an African w horse with stripes.

zero
Zero is nothing, none,

zigzag
A line with sharp angle If you travel in a zigza you move suddenly fro side to side.

zipper
A zipper has two sets metal or plastic teeth th grip each other and fast things together.

zoo
A zoo is the place to see kinds of different anima Most of the animals are k in enclosures or cages